THE LOST RACE

BY

ROBERT E. HOWARD

British Library Cataloguing-in-Publication Data
A catalogue record for this book is available from the
British Library

Robert E. Howard

Robert Ervin Howard was born in Peaster, Texas in 1906. During his youth, his family moved between a variety of Texan boomtowns, and Howard – a bookish and somewhat introverted child – was steeped in the violent myths and legends of the Old South. Although he loved reading and learning, Howard developed a distinctly Texan, hardboiled outlook on the world. He became a passionate fan of boxing, taking it up at an amateur level, and from the age of nine began to write adventure tales of semi-historical bloodshed. In 1919, when Howard was thirteen, his family moved to the Central Texas hamlet of Cross Plains, where he would stay for the rest of his life.

At fifteen Howard began to read the pulp magazines of the day, and to write more seriously. The December 1922 issue of his high school newspaper featured two of his stories, 'Golden Hope Christmas' and 'West is West'. In 1924 he sold his first piece – a short caveman tale titled 'Spear and Fang' – for $16 to the not-yet-famous *Weird Tales* magazine. He published with the magazine regularly over the next few years. 1929 was a breakout year for Howard, in that the 23-year-old writer began to sell to other magazines, such as *Ghost Stories* and *Argosy*, both of whom had previously sent him hundreds of rejection slips. In 1930, he began a correspondence with weird fiction master H. P. Lovecraft which ran up to his death six years later, and is regarded as one of the great correspondence cycles in all of fantasy literature.

It was partly due to Lovecraft's encouragement that Howard created his most famous character, Conan the Cimmerian. Conan – a barbarian-turned-King during the Hyborian Age, a mythical period of some 12,000 years ago – featured in seventeen *Weird Tales* stories between 1933 and 1936, and is now regarded as having spawned the 'sword and sorcery' genre, making Howard's influence on fantasy literature comparable to that of J. R. R. Tolkien's. The Conan stories have since been adapted many times, most famously in the series of films starring Arnold Schwarzenegger.

Howard was enjoying an all-time high in sales by the beginning of 1936, but he was also deeply upset by the ill health of his mother, who had fallen into a coma. On the morning of June 11, 1936, he asked an attending nurse whether she would ever recover, and the nurse replied negatively. Howard walked to his car, parked outside the family home in Cross Plains, and shot himself. He died eight hours later, aged just thirty.

Cororuc glanced about him and hastened his pace. He was no coward, but he did not like the place. Tall trees rose all about, their sullen branches shutting out the sunlight. The dim trail led in and out among them, sometimes skirting the edge of a ravine, where Cororuc could gaze down at the treetops beneath. Occasionally, through a rift in the forest, he could see away to the forbidding hills that hinted of the ranges much farther to the west, that were the mountains of Cornwall.

In those mountains the bandit chief, Buruc the Cruel, was supposed to lurk, to descend upon such victims as might pass that way. Cororuc shifted his grip on his spear and quickened his step. His haste was due not only to the menace of the outlaws, but also to the fact that he wished once more to be in his native land. He had been on a secret mission to the wild Cornish tribesmen; and though he had been more or less successful, he was impatient to be out of their inhospitable country. It had been a long, wearisome trip, and he still had nearly the whole of Britain to traverse. He threw a glance of aversion about him. He longed for the pleasant woodlands, with scampering deer, and chirping birds, to which he was used. He longed for the tall white cliff, where the blue sea lapped merrily. The forest through which he was passing seemed uninhabited. There were no birds, no animals; nor had he seen a sign of human habitation.

His comrades still lingered at the savage court of the Cornish king, enjoying his crude hospitality, in no hurry to be away. But Cororuc was not content. So he had left them to follow at their leisure and had set out alone.

Rather a fine figure of a man was Cororuc. Some six feet in height, strongly though leanly built, he was, with gray eyes, a pure Briton but not a pure Celt, his long yellow hair revealing, in him as in all his race, a trace of Belgae.

He was clad in skillfully dressed deerskin, for the Celts had not yet perfected the coarse cloth which they made, and most of the race preferred the hides of deer.

He was armed with a long bow of yew wood, made with no especial skill but an efficient weapon; a long bronze broadsword, with a buckskin sheath; a long bronze dagger and a small, round shield, rimmed with a band of bronze and covered with tough buffalo hide. A crude bronze helmet was on his head. Faint devices were painted in woad on his arms and cheeks.

His beardless face was of the highest type of Briton, clear, straightforward, the shrewd, practical determination of the Nordic mingling with the reckless courage and dreamy artistry of the Celt.

So Cororuc trod the forest path, warily, ready to flee or fight, but preferring to do neither just then.

The trail led away from the ravine, disappearing around a great tree. And from the other side of the tree, Cororuc heard sounds of conflict. Gliding warily forward, and wondering whether he should see some of the elves and dwarfs that were reputed to haunt those woodlands, he peered around the great tree.

A few feet from him he saw a strange tableau. Backed against another tree stood a large wolf, at bay, blood trickling from gashes about his shoulder; while before him, crouching for a spring, the warrior saw a great panther. Cororuc wondered at the cause of the battle. Not often the lords of the forest met in warfare. And he was puzzled by the snarls of the great cat. Savage, blood-lusting, yet they held a strange note of fear; and the beast seemed hesitant to spring in.

Just why Cororuc chose to take the part of the wolf, he himself could not have said. Doubtless it was just the reckless chivalry of the Celt in him, an admiration for the dauntless attitude of the wolf against his far more powerful foe. Be that as it may, Cororuc, characteristically forgetting his bow and taking the more reckless course, drew his sword and leaped in front of the panther. But he had no chance to use it. The panther, whose nerve appeared to be already somewhat shaken, uttered a startled screech and disappeared among the trees so quickly that Cororuc wondered if he had really seen a panther. He turned to the wolf, wondering if it would leap upon him. It was watching him, half crouching; slowly it stepped away from the tree, and still watching him, backed away a few yards, then turned and made off with a strange shambling gait. As the warrior watched it vanish into the forest, an uncanny feeling came over him; he had seen many wolves, he had hunted them and had been hunted by them, but he had never seen such a wolf before.

He hesitated and then walked warily after the wolf, following the tracks that were plainly defined in the soft loam. He did not hasten, being merely content to follow the tracks. After a short distance, he stopped short, the hairs on his neck seeming to bristle. Only the tracks of the hind feet showed: the wolf was walking erect.

He glanced about him. There was no sound; the forest was silent. He felt an impulse to turn and put as much territory between him and the mystery as possible, but his Celtic curiosity would not allow it. He followed the trail. And then it ceased altogether. Beneath a great tree the tracks vanished. Cororuc felt the cold sweat on his forehead. What kind of place was that forest? Was he being led astray and eluded by some inhuman, supernatural monster of the woodlands, who sought to ensnare him? And Cororuc backed away, his sword lifted, his courage not allowing him to run, but greatly desiring to do so. And so he came again to the tree where he had first seen the wolf. The trail he had followed led away from it in another direction and Cororuc took it up, almost running in his haste to get out of the vicinity of a wolf who walked on two legs and then vanished in the air.

The trail wound about more tediously than ever, appearing and disappearing within a dozen feet, but it was well for Cororuc that it did, for thus he heard the voices of the men coming up the path before they saw him. He took to a tall tree that branched over the trail, lying close to the great bole, along a wide-flung branch.

Three men were coming down the forest path.

One was a big, burly fellow, vastly over six feet in height, with a long red beard and a great mop of red hair. In contrast, his eyes were a beady black. He was dressed in deerskins, and armed with a great sword.

Of the two others, one was a lanky, villainous-looking scoundrel, with only one eye, and the other was a small, wizened man, who squinted hideously with both beady eyes.

Cororuc knew them, by descriptions the Cornishmen had made between curses, and it was in his excitement to get a better view of the most villainous murderer in Britain that he slipped from the tree branch and plunged to the ground directly between them.

He was up on the instant, his sword out. He could expect no mercy; for he knew that the red-haired man was Buruc the Cruel, the scourge of Cornwall.

The bandit chief bellowed a foul curse and whipped out his great sword. He avoided the Briton's furious thrust by a swift backward leap and then the battle was on. Buruc rushed the warrior from the front, striving to beat him down by sheer weight; while the lanky, one-eyed villain slipped around, trying to get behind him. The smaller man had retreated to the edge of the forest. The fine art of the fence was unknown to those early swordsmen. It was hack, slash, stab, the full weight of the arm behind each blow. The terrific blows crashing on his shield beat Cororuc to the ground, and the lanky, one-eyed villain rushed in to finish him. Cororuc spun about without rising, cut the bandit's legs from under him and stabbed him as he fell, then threw himself to one side and to his feet, in time to avoid Buruc's sword. Again, driving his shield up to catch the bandit's sword in midair, he deflected it and whirled his own with all his power. Buruc's head flew from his shoulders.

Then Cororuc, turning, saw the wizened bandit scurry into the forest. He raced after him, but the fellow had disappeared among the trees. Knowing the uselessness of attempting to pursue him, Cororuc turned and raced down the trail. He did not know if there were more bandits in that direction, but he did know that if he expected to get out of the forest at all, he would have to do it swiftly. Without doubt the villain who had escaped would have all the other bandits out, and soon they would be beating the woodlands for him.

After running for some distance down the path and seeing no sign of any enemy, he stopped and climbed into the topmost branches of a tall tree that towered above its fellows.

On all sides he seemed surrounded by a leafy ocean. To the west he could see the hills he had avoided. To the north, far in the distance, other hills rose; to the south the forest ran, an unbroken sea. But to the east, far away, he could barely see the line that marked the thinning out of the forest into the fertile plains. Miles and miles away, he knew not how many, but it meant more pleasant travel, villages of men, people of his own race. He was surprized that he was able to see that far, but the tree in which he stood was a giant of its kind.

Before he started to descend, he glanced about nearer at hand. He could trace the faintly marked line of the trail he had been following, running away into the east; and could make out other trails leading into it, or away from it. Then a glint caught his eye. He fixed his gaze on a glade some distance down the trail and saw, presently, a party of men enter and vanish. Here and there, on every trail, he caught glances of the glint of accouterments, the waving of foliage. So the squinting villain had already roused the bandits. They were all around him; he was virtually surrounded.

A faintly heard burst of savage yells, from back up the trail, startled him. So, they had already thrown a cordon about the place of the fight and had found him gone. Had he not fled swiftly, he would have been caught. He was outside the cordon, but the bandits were all about him. Swiftly he slipped from the tree and glided into the forest.

Then began the most exciting hunt Cororuc had ever engaged in; for he was the hunted and men were the hunters. Gliding, slipping from bush to bush and from tree to tree, now running swiftly, now crouching in a covert, Cororuc fled, ever eastward, not daring to turn back lest he be driven farther back into the forest. At times he was forced to turn his course; in fact, he very seldom fled in a straight course, yet always he managed to work farther eastward.

Sometimes he crouched in bushes or lay along some leafy branch, and saw bandits pass so close to him that he could have touched them. Once or twice they sighted him and he fled, bounding over logs and bushes, darting in and out among the trees; and always he eluded them.

It was in one of those headlong flights that he noticed he had entered a defile of small hills, of which he had been unaware, and looking back over his shoulder, saw that his pursuers had halted, within full sight. Without pausing to ruminate on so strange a thing, he darted around a great boulder, felt a vine or something catch his foot, and was thrown headlong. Simultaneously, something struck the youth's head, knocking him senseless.

When Cororuc recovered his senses, he found that he was bound, hand and foot. He was being borne along, over rough ground. He looked about him. Men carried him on their shoulders, but such men as he had never seen before. Scarce above four feet stood the tallest, and they were small of build and very dark of complexion. Their eyes were black; and most of them went stooped forward, as if from a lifetime spent in crouching and hiding; peering furtively on all sides. They were armed with small bows, arrows, spears and daggers, all pointed, not with crudely worked bronze but with flint and obsidian, of the finest workmanship. They were dressed in finely dressed hides of rabbits and other small animals, and a kind of coarse cloth; and many were tattooed from head to foot in ocher and woad. There were perhaps twenty in all. What sort of men were they? Cororuc had never seen the like.

They were going down a ravine, on both sides of which steep cliffs rose. Presently they seemed to come to a blank wall, where the ravine appeared to come to an abrupt stop. Here, at a word from one who seemed to be in command, they set the Briton down, and seizing hold of a large boulder, drew it to one side. A small cavern was exposed, seeming to vanish away into the earth; then the strange men picked up the Briton and moved forward.

Cororuc's hair bristled at the thought of being borne into that forbidding-looking cave. What manner of men were they? In all Britain and Alba, in Cornwall or Ireland, Cororuc had never seen such men. Small dwarfish men, who dwelt in the earth. Cold sweat broke out on the youth's forehead. Surely they were the malevolent dwarfs of whom the Cornish people had spoken, who dwelt in their caverns by day, and by night sallied forth to steal and burn dwellings, even slaying if the opportunity arose! You will hear of them, even today, if you journey in Cornwall.

The men, or elves, if such they were, bore him into the cavern, others entering and drawing the boulder back into place. For a moment all was darkness, and then torches began to glow, away off. And at a shout they moved on. Other men of the caves came forward, with the torches.

Cororuc looked about him. The torches shed a vague glow over the scene. Sometimes one, sometimes another wall of the cave showed for an instant, and the Briton was vaguely aware that they were covered with paintings, crudely done, yet with a certain skill his own race could not equal. But always the roof remained unseen. Cororuc knew that the seemingly small cavern had merged into a cave of surprizing size. Through the vague light of the torches the strange people moved, came and went, silently, like shadows of the dim past.

He felt the cords of thongs that bound his feet loosened. He was lifted upright.

"Walk straight ahead," said a voice, speaking the language of his own race, and he felt a spear point touch the back of his neck.

And straight ahead he walked, feeling his sandals scrape on the stone floor of the cave, until they came to a place where the floor tilted upward. The pitch was steep and the stone was so slippery that Cororuc could not have climbed it alone. But his captors pushed him, and pulled him, and he saw that long, strong vines were strung from somewhere at the top.

Those the strange men seized, and bracing their feet against the slippery ascent, went up swiftly. When their feet found level surface again, the cave made a turn, and Cororuc blundered out into a fire-lit scene that made him gasp.

The cave debouched into a cavern so vast as to be almost incredible. The mighty walls swept up into a great arched roof that vanished in the darkness. A level floor lay between, and through it flowed a river; an underground river. From under one wall it flowed to vanish silently under the other. An arched stone bridge, seemingly of natural make, spanned the current.

All around the walls of the great cavern, which was roughly circular, were smaller caves, and before each glowed a fire. Higher up were other caves, regularly arranged, tier on tier. Surely human men could not have built such a city.

In and out among the caves, on the level floor of the main cavern, people were going about what seemed daily tasks. Men were talking together and mending weapons, some were fishing from the river; women were replenishing fires, preparing garments; and altogether it might have been any other village in Britain, to judge from their occupations. But it all struck Cororuc as extremely unreal; the strange place, the small, silent people, going about their tasks, the river flowing silently through it all.

Then they became aware of the prisoner and flocked about him. There was none of the shouting, abuse and indignities, such as savages usually heap on their captives, as the small men drew about Cororuc, silently eying him with malevolent, wolfish stares. The warrior shuddered, in spite of himself.

But his captors pushed through the throng, driving the Briton before them. Close to the bank of the river, they stopped and drew away from around him.

Two great fires leaped and flickered in front of him and there was something between them. He focused his gaze and presently made out the object. A high stone seat, like a throne; and in it seated an aged man, with a long white beard, silent, motionless, but with black eyes that gleamed like a wolf's.

The ancient was clothed in some kind of a single, flowing garment. One claw-like hand rested on the seat near him, skinny, crooked fingers, with talons like a hawk's. The other hand was hidden among his garments.

The firelight danced and flickered; now the old man stood out clearly, his hooked, beak-like nose and long beard thrown into bold relief; now he seemed to recede until he was invisible to the gaze of the Briton, except for his glittering eyes.

"Speak, Briton!" The words came suddenly, strong, clear, without a hint of age. "Speak, what would ye say?"

Cororuc, taken aback, stammered and said, "Why, why--what manner people are you? Why have you taken me prisoner? Are you elves?"

"We are Picts," was the stern reply.

"Picts!" Cororuc had heard tales of those ancient people from the Gaelic Britons; some said that they still lurked in the hills of Siluria, but--

"I have fought Picts in Caledonia," the Briton protested; "they are short but massive and misshapen; not at all like you!"

"They are not true Picts," came the stern retort. "Look about you, Briton," with a wave of an arm, "you see the remnants of a vanishing race; a race that once ruled Britain from sea to sea."

The Briton stared, bewildered.

"Harken, Briton," the voice continued; "harken, barbarian, while I tell to you the tale of the lost race."

The firelight flickered and danced, throwing vague reflections on the towering walls and on the rushing, silent current.

The ancient's voice echoed through the mighty cavern.

"Our people came from the south. Over the islands, over the Inland Sea. Over the snow-topped mountains, where some remained, to slay any enemies who might follow. Down into the fertile plains we came. Over all the land we spread. We became wealthy and prosperous. Then two kings arose in the land, and he who conquered, drove out the conquered. So many of us made boats and set sail for the far-off cliffs that gleamed white in the sunlight. We found a fair land with fertile plains. We found a race of red-haired barbarians, who dwelt in caves. Mighty giants, of great bodies and small minds.

"We built our huts of wattle. We tilled the soil. We cleared the forest. We drove the red-haired giants back into the forest. Farther we drove them back until at last they fled to the mountains of the west and the mountains of the north. We were rich. We were prosperous.

"Then," and his voice thrilled with rage and hate, until it seemed to reverberate through the cavern, "then the Celts came. From the isles of the west, in their rude coracles they came. In the west they landed, but they were not satisfied with the west. They marched eastward and seized the fertile plains. We fought. They were stronger. They were fierce fighters and they were armed with weapons of bronze, whereas we had only weapons of flint.

"We were driven out. They enslaved us. They drove us into the forest. Some of us fled into the mountains of the west. Many fled into the mountains of the north. There they mingled with the red-haired giants we drove out so long ago, and became a race of monstrous dwarfs, losing all the arts of peace and gaining only the ability to fight.

"But some of us swore that we would never leave the land we had fought for. But the Celts pressed us. There were many, and more came. So we took to caverns, to ravines, to caves. We, who had always dwelt in huts that let in much light, who had always tilled the soil, we learned to dwell like beasts, in caves where no sunlight ever entered. Caves we found, of which this is the greatest; caves we made.

"You, Briton," the voice became a shriek and a long arm was outstretched in accusation, "you and your race! You have made a free, prosperous nation into a race of earth-rats! We who never fled, who dwelt in the air and the sunlight close by the sea where traders came, we must flee like hunted beasts and burrow like moles! But at night! Ah, then for our vengeance! Then we slip from our hiding places, ravines and caves, with torch and dagger! Look, Briton!"

And following the gesture, Cororuc saw a rounded post of some kind of very hard wood, set in a niche in the stone floor, close to the bank. The floor about the niche was charred as if by old fires.

Cororuc stared, uncomprehending. Indeed, he understood little of what had passed. That these people were even human, he was not at all certain. He had heard so

17

much of them as "little people." Tales of their doings, their hatred of the race of man, and their maliciousness flocked back to him. Little he knew that he was gazing on one of the mysteries of the ages. That the tales which the ancient Gaels told of the Picts, already warped, would become even more warped from age to age, to result in tales of elves, dwarfs, trolls and fairies, at first accepted and then rejected, entire, by the race of men, just as the Neanderthal monsters resulted in tales of goblins and ogres. But of that Cororuc neither knew nor cared, and the ancient was speaking again.

"There, there, Briton," exulted he, pointing to the post, "there you shall pay! A scant payment for the debt your race owes mine, but to the fullest of your extent."

The old man's exultation would have been fiendish, except for a certain high purpose in his face. He was sincere. He believed that he was only taking just vengeance; and he seemed like some great patriot for a mighty, lost cause.

"But I am a Briton!" stammered Cororuc. "It was not my people who drove your race into exile! They were Gaels, from Ireland. I am a Briton and my race came from Gallia only a hundred years ago. We conquered the Gaels and drove them into Erin, Wales and Caledonia, even as they drove your race."

"No matter!" The ancient chief was on his feet. "A Celt is a Celt. Briton, or Gael, it makes no difference. Had it not been Gael, it would have been Briton. Every Celt who falls into our hands must pay, be it warrior or woman, babe or king. Seize him and bind him to the post."

In an instant Cororuc was bound to the post, and he saw, with horror, the Picts piling firewood about his feet.

"And when you are sufficiently burned, Briton," said the ancient, "this dagger that has drunk the blood of a hundred Britons, shall quench its thirst in yours."

"But never have I harmed a Pict!" Cororuc gasped, struggling with his bonds.

"You pay, not for what you did, but for what your race has done," answered the ancient sternly. "Well do I remember the deeds of the Celts when first they landed on Britain--the shrieks of the slaughtered, the screams of ravished girls, the smokes of burning villages, the plundering."

Cororuc felt his short neck-hairs bristle. When first the Celts landed on Britain! That was over five hundred years ago!

And his Celtic curiosity would not let him keep still, even at the stake with the Picts preparing to light firewood piled about him.

"You could not remember that. That was ages ago."

The ancient looked at him somberly. "And I am age-old. In my youth I was a witch-finder, and an old woman witch cursed me as she writhed at the stake. She said I should live until the last child of the Pictish race had passed. That I should see the once mighty nation go down into oblivion and then--and only then--should I follow it. For she put upon me the curse of life everlasting."

Then his voice rose until it filled the cavern. "But the curse was nothing. Words can do no harm, can do nothing, to a man. I live. A hundred generations have I seen come and go, and yet another hundred. What is time? The sun rises and sets, and another day has passed into oblivion. Men watch the sun and set their lives by it. They league themselves on every hand with time. They count the minutes that race them into eternity. Man outlived the centuries ere he began to reckon time. Time is man-made. Eternity is the work of the gods. In this cavern there is no such thing as time. There are no stars, no sun. Without is time; within is eternity. We count not time. Nothing marks the speeding of the hours. The youths go forth. They see the sun, the stars. They reckon time. And they pass. I was a young man when I entered this cavern. I have never left it. As you reckon time, I may have dwelt here a thousand years; or an hour. When not banded by time, the soul, the mind, call it what you will, can conquer the body. And the wise men of the race, in my youth, knew more than the outer world will ever learn. When I feel that my body begins to weaken, I take the magic draft, that is known only to me, of all the world. It does not give immortality; that is the work of the mind alone; but it rebuilds the body. The race of Picts vanish; they fade like the snow on the mountain. And when the last is gone, this dagger shall free me from the world." Then in a swift change of tone, "Light the fagots!"

Cororuc's mind was fairly reeling. He did not in the least understand what he had just heard. He was positive that he was going mad; and what he saw the next minute assured him of it.

Through the throng came a wolf; and he knew that it was the wolf whom he had rescued from the panther close by the ravine in the forest!

Strange, how long ago and far away that seemed! Yes, it was the same wolf. That same strange, shambling gait. Then the thing stood erect and raised its front feet to its head. What nameless horror was that?

Then the wolf's head fell back, disclosing a man's face. The face of a Pict; one of the first "werewolves." The man stepped out of the wolfskin and strode forward, calling something. A Pict just starting to light the wood about the Briton's feet drew back the torch and hesitated.

The wolf-Pict stepped forward and began to speak to the chief, using Celtic, evidently for the prisoner's benefit. Cororuc was surprised to hear so many speak his language, not reflecting upon its comparative simplicity, and the ability of the Picts.

"What is this?" asked the Pict who had played wolf. "A man is to be burned who should not be!"

"How?" exclaimed the old man fiercely, clutching his long beard. "Who are you to go against a custom of age-old antiquity?"

"I met a panther," answered the other, "and this Briton risked his life to save mine. Shall a Pict show ingratitude?"

And as the ancient hesitated, evidently pulled one way by his fanatical lust for revenge, and the other by his equally fierce racial pride, the Pict burst into a wild flight of oration, carried on in his own language. At last the ancient chief nodded.

"A Pict ever paid his debts," said he with impressive grandeur. "Never a Pict forgets. Unbind him. No Celt shall ever say that a Pict showed ingratitude."

Cororuc was released, and as, like a man in a daze, he tried to stammer his thanks, the chief waved them aside.

"A Pict never forgets a foe, ever remembers a friendly deed," he replied.

"Come," murmured his Pictish friend, tugging at the Celt's arm.

He led the way into a cave leading away from the main cavern. As they went, Cororuc looked back, to see the ancient chief seated upon his stone throne, his eyes gleaming as he seemed to gaze back through the lost glories of the ages; on each hand the fires leaped and flickered. A figure of grandeur, the king of a lost race.

On and on Cororuc's guide led him. And at last they emerged and the Briton saw the starlit sky above him.

"In that way is a village of your tribesmen," said the Pict, pointing, "where you will find a welcome until you wish to take up your journey anew."

And he pressed gifts on the Celt; gifts of garments of cloth and finely worked deerskin, beaded belts, a fine horn bow with arrows skillfully tipped with obsidian. Gifts of food. His own weapons were returned to him.

"But an instant," said the Briton, as the Pict turned to go. "I followed your tracks in the forest. They vanished." There was a question in his voice.

The Pict laughed softly. "I leaped into the branches of the tree. Had you looked up, you would have seen me. If ever you wish a friend, you will ever find one in Berula, chief among the Alban Picts."

He turned and vanished. And Cororuc strode through the moonlight toward the Celtic village.

THE END